The DAY
the CRAYONS
came HOME

To my parents,

Charles and Charlene Daywalt,

who taught me to always make room for everyone.

—D.D.

For Logan.

—O.J.

The DAY the CRAYONS came HOME

DREW DAYWALT   OLIVER JEFFERS

HarperCollins *Children's Books*

One day, Duncan and his crayons were happily colouring together when a strange stack of postcards arrived for him in the mail . . .

Dear Duncan,

Not sure if you remember me. My name is MAROON CRAYON. You only coloured with me once, to draw a scab, but whatever. Anyway, you LOST me TWO years ago in the couch, then your Dad SAT on me and BROKE ME IN HALF! I never would have SURVIVED had PAPERCLIP not NURSED me back to Health. I'm finally better, so come and get me! And can Paper Clip come too? He's really holding me together.

Sincerely,
Your marooned crayon,
MAROON CRAYON

Published by Coleman Ltd., Printed in the Republic of Ireland.

434

BELFAST

POSTAGE THE COU

20 15

4p

DUNCAN

Duncan's Bedroom

UPSTAIRS

THIS HOUSE

POSTAGE IN SIDE 2015

DR-29304-B

post card

Dear Duncan,
No one likes peas.
No one even likes the colour
PEA GREEN.   So I'm changing
my name and RUNNing away
to see the WORLD.

Sincerely,
Esteban... the MAGNIFIcent!
(the Crayon formerly known as .PEA GREEN)

DUNCAN
DUNCAN's BEDroom
upstairs
This HOUSE

Hi DUNCAN,   **RITZ MOTEL**
          A lovely spot for year 'round recreation

It's me, NEON RED crayon.
REMEMBER that great holiday we
had with your family? Remember
how we laughed when we drew a
picture of your Dad's SUNBURN?
Remember dropping me by the hotel
pool when you left? Clearly you
do NOT, BECAUSE I'M STILL HERE!
How could you miss me? Anyway.
After 8 months waiting for you to come
and get me, I guess I'm walking BACK...

          Your left-behind friend,
          NEON RED CRAYON

POSTAGE LOST 2015

AIR TRAVEL
3¢
THREE

POST CARD

Duncan
Duncan's Room
Duncan's House

PICKING COCONUTS
FUN IN THE SUN !

Duncan!
It's us... Yellow and ORANge. we know
we used to ARgue over which of us
was the colour of the SUN... But GUESS
what? NEITHER of us wants to be
the COLOUR of the SUN any more. Not since
we were LEFT OUTSIDE and the SUN
MELTED us... TOGETHER!! You
know the REAL colour of the SUN??
HOT. That's what. We're sorry for
arguing. You can make GREEN the
sun for all we care, just BRING
US HOME!

Your not-so-sunny friends,
Yellow & ORANge

AIR MAIL

OUT SIDE
2015
POSTAGE

SPACE
USA
34c

Post Card

Duncan

Duncan's room

INSIDE!

That House

there →

Hey Duncan, **Greetings from**
NARROWSBURG
I'm sure you don't recognise me...
after the horrors I've been through.
I think I was... Tan CRAYON?
or maybe... Burnt sienna? I don't
know...I can't tell any more. Have
you ever been eaten by a dog and puked
up on the living room rug? Because
I have... I <u>HAVE</u> BEEN EATEN BY A DOG
AND PUKED UP ON THE RUG, Duncan...
and it's <u>NOT</u> pretty. Not pretty at all...
I'm more carpet fuzz than crayon now.
Can you PLEASE bring me back?!

Your INDIGESTIBLE friend,
Tan (or possibly Burnt Sienna?) Crayon

P4135

Post Card
ADDRESS

Duncan

His Bedroom

Upstairs

POSTAGE
2015
THE DOOR

BROCCOLI

6p.

Dearest Duncan,

um... could you please
OPEN the FRONT DOOR?
I still need to see
the world...

sincerely,
Esteban the
Magnificent

Post Card

Duncan

Duncan's Bedroom
Upstairs
This House

Rev. 1-4

Hey Duncan,
Remember last Halloween we told
your little brother there was a
GHOST under the BASEMENT stairs?
Then we drew that SCARY stuff on
the wall? Sure was funny when he ran
SCREAMING, right? But It wasn't so
funny when you FORGOT to take
me out of the BASEMENT! Please
come and get me!
I'm   kind   of... terribly...   horrified...

Your   scared   friend,
gLOW in the DARK crayon

DUNCan
Duncan's
   Bedroom
UPStairs
THIS   HOUSE

POST CARD

Glow in the dark

Dear DUNCan,

Looks like I'm almost home!
Been through China, Canada and
France... I think.
Just crossing Newcastle
by camel now!
Newcastle has GIANT
pyramids, right?

See ya soon,
Neon RED Crayon

P.S. Next stop, the NORth Pole
(I think)

POSTAGE
OUT
SIDE
2 0 1 5

22ε

DUNCan
Duncan's Room
DUNCAN'S HOUSE

The Land of Gold

Duncan,
Does page 8 of "PIRATE ISland" ring a bell?
Kind of a big payday for CAPtain GREENBeard
there, don't ya think? And NO BRONZE
or silver in that pile, huh? I told
you it'd make me blunt if you
coloured each coin INDIVIDUALLy, But
would you Listen? NOoo.
I Also told you those stupid crayon
sharpeners NEVER WORK. Did you
Listen to that? Also NOOoo.
NOW I can't colour ANYthing at ALL!

    Your Pointless FRiend,
    GOLD CRAYon

POST CARD

Duncan
DUNCAN'S ROOM
UPStairs

I HAD to write it for him.

This IS NOT FUN For ME either, you KNow!

A Haul of Loot

A Bad Day for the Cabin Boy

Dear Duncan,

I've seen the world.
It's rainy.
I'm coming back.

Esteban
   the MAGNIFicent

POST CARD

MULHOLLAND PRESS, INC.

POSTAGE 2015 THE DOOR

EXPLORER 23

TO Duncan
   Duncan's Bedroom
   Upstairs
   This House

#72-26 PASSING OF THE STORM...

M
P

Hi DUNCAN,

You're probably wondering why my head is stuck to Your SOCK? A question I ask myself every DAY. Well... it's because last week you left me in your pocket and I ended up in the DRYER. I landed on your sock and now he's stuck to my head. Can you please come and get me? Also, why does everything you wear still smell even after it's washed?

Your stinky-socky-stucky-
  on-head buddy,
  TURQUOISE Crayon
  P.S. Sock says "Hi"

The awesome splendor of a thundering waterfall.

PHOTO BY: S. DACEY ® COLOR REPRODUCTION (REG. U.S.A. PAT. OFF.)

POST CARD

POSTAGE
DOWN
STAIRS
20 LOST 5

DUCKIE
26

DUNCAN
Duncan's
  Room
Upstairs

Dear Mr Duncan,

I know I'm not your crayon. I know I belong to your Baby Brother, but I can't TAKE him any more. In the last WEEK alone he's bitten the TOP of my HEAD, put me in the cat's NOSE, drawn on the WALL and tried to colour RUBBISH with me! The WORST part is he is a TERRIBLE Artist! I can't tell what his drawings are. Donkeys? Monkeys? DONKEY-MONKEYS? Picasso said every child is an artist, but I dunno. I don't think he met your Brother. Please Rescue me.

Your desperate Friend,
BIG CHUNKY Toddler Crayon

CARTE POSTALE

ADRESSE

M Duncan
Duncan's Room
Upstairs
This House

SKIING AND A FAST JUMP ALONG THE TRAIL

Duncan,
greetings from the
AMAZON Rainforest.

Making GREat TIME!
I think I'm almost home.

NEON RED crayon

Pub. by Maeve S. White Ridge Enterprise, 04102

OUTSIDE POSTAGE 2015

4¢ WINTER

DR-28060-B

post card

Duncan
DUNCAN's Room
DUNCan's House

Sp MADE BY SCAMPI PRESS

Hello Duncan,

It's me, BROWN Crayon. You know
EXACTly why I ran away, buddy!
Everyone thinks I get ALL the great colouring
jobs - chocolate, puppies, ponies. Lucky me,
right? Bet they don't know what Else you
used me to colour, do they? I didn't think so.
The rest of that drawing was great,
but did it really need that FINAL
BROWN scribble?
I'll come back, but please let's
stick to CHOCOLATE, ok?

Your VERY embarrassed Friend,
BROWN   CRAYON

IN THE MAINE WOODS

POST CARD

Duncan
DUNCAN'S ROOM
DUNCAN'S House
Next DOOR

VACATIONLAND
35¢
USA
Postage

INSIDE
2015
POSTAGE

"BEAR GOES in the WOODS" by Duncan

Hey Duncan,
I'm sure you don't recognise me...
after the horrors I've been through.
I think I was... Tan CRAYON?
or maybe... Burnt Sienna? I don't
know... I can't tell any more. Have
you ever been eaten by a dog and puked
up on the living room rug? Because
I have... I HAVE BEEN EATEN BY A DOG
AND PUKED UP ON THE RUG, Duncan.
and it's NOT pretty. Not pretty at all...
I'm more carpet fuzz than crayon now.
can you PLEASE bring me back?!
Your INDIGESTIBLE friend,
Tan (or possibly Burnt Sienna?) Crayon

POSTAGE
DOWNSTAIRS
2015

Post Card
ADDRESS

Duncan
His Bed
UPSTA

P4135

MULHOLLAND PRESS, INC.

Dear Duncan,
Not sure if you remember me. my n
MAROON CRAYON. You only col
once, to draw a scab, but what
you LOST me TWO years
couch, then your Dad SAT o
BROKE ME IN HALF
ever would have SURVIVED ha
PER clip not NURSED me
alth. I'm finall
get me!

Western
SUN

How
After 8 m
and get me, I gu

Your left-o
NEON RED CR

THE MOTEL
N
Playground
Volcano
North Pole
Air-Conditioning
Swimming Pool
Free Radios
Saturn
Duncan's Room

ADRESSE
POSTAGE
2015
INSIDE

Duncan
Duncan's Room
UPSTAIRS
THIS House

CARTE POSTALE

الجيزة - الأهرامات
GIZA - The Pyramide

P.S
RED Crayon
Next stop, the NORTH POLE
(I think)

DUNCAN

Dear Mr Duncan,

Duncan was sad to learn of all the crayons he'd lost, forgotten, broken or neglected over the years. So he ran around gathering them up.

But Duncan's crayons were all so damaged and differently shaped than they used to be that they no longer fitted in the crayon box.

So Duncan had an idea . . .

He built a place where each crayon
would *always* feel at home.

ALSO BY DREW DAYWALT AND OLIVER JEFFERS:

The Day the Crayons Quit

First published in the USA by Philomel Books, an imprint of Penguin Young Readers Group, in 2015
First published in hardback in Great Britain by HarperCollins Children's Books in 2015
First published in paperback in 2016

1 3 5 7 9 10 8 6 4 2

ISBN: 978-0-00-812444-1

HarperCollins Children's Books is a division of HarperCollins Publishers Ltd.

Text copyright © Drew Daywalt 2015
Illustrations copyright © Oliver Jeffers 2015
Published by arrangement with Philomel, a division of Penguin Young Readers Group, Penguin Group (USA) LLC

Visit our website at: www.harpercollins.co.uk

Printed in China

Edited by Michael Green. The artwork for this book was made with crayons, the Postal Service and a cardboard box.

GREETINGS FROM NEITHER HERE NOR TH...

POST·CARD

PLACE
STAMP
HERE

AP 10 *CRAYON POSTCARD. MADE BY ME*

THE CRAYON CASTLE

1 Mile west of Duncan's Bedroom. Left out of the Garage.

CRAYON INN MOTEL

Need to Get Out of the Box? Enjoy Our Air Conditioned Suites!

RESTAURANT LOUNGE

Wish you were here

Also look out for these brilliant picture books!